T0354715

THE
TREE CLIMBER

THE TREE CLIMBER

RAYMOND C. WOOD

THE TREE CLIMBER

iUniverse books may be ordered through booksellers or by contacting:

iUniverse
1663 Liberty Drive
Bloomington, IN 47403
www.iuniverse.com
844-349-9409

ISBN: 978-1-6632-6913-3 (sc)
ISBN: 978-1-6632-6914-0 (e)

Print information available on the last page.

iUniverse rev. date: 12/09/2024

PREFACE

While working for a tree company, Jeff Standish was on top of a high Ash tree where he could see the third-floor terrace. It was there that he saw the interrupted assault of a young girl, followed by the flight of a man down the fire escape and into a car that exactly matched his brother-in-law's!

CHAPTER ONE

As the June sun rose over the small town of Seaburg 30 miles south of Boston, Jeff Standish emerged from his apartment to head for his job on the edge of town. Although at times working for a tree company could be grueling work, he loved the fact that the money was good and always relished working outdoors and with his hands. Working indoors or behind a desk just wouldn't have suited him in the least.

Arriving at the Cedar Post Tree Company barn, he joined a three-man crew to fell a tree in the adjoining town of Kemper. Jeff alighted his older Ford pickup and joined the foreman, Bert, and Irishman, Casey, who had a distinctive Irish brogue and held the company's current record for highest climb, going beyond the 120-feet of rope and free-climbing another 35 feet to the top of a big oak tree. The last of the trio was Sam Parker, a dark-skinned feller from Kemper who, at 28, was the same age as Jeff. The two took an instant liking to one another when they first met and usually went to a small tavern in Seaburg to have a few beers and unwind whenever they finally left the so-called barn for the day. The barn, of course, was where all their trucks and equipment were kept.

As they were pulling out the dump truck and the Dodge crew cab, Bert walked over to Jeff.

"Jeff," he spoke, "I want you to top the Ash tree. I think Casey had one too many last night. He won't admit it, but I don't want him climbing."

"Okay, no problem. I'll grab my rope and saddle."

"This is a take-down where the owner wants all the wood, so it should go rather smoothly. We'll just bring the dump and the chipper," Bert added.

Soon they arrived at the job site. Jeff could see that the tree was next to a three-story apartment building that the owner wanted to expand. Donning his harness, he footlocked up around 10 feet to the highest branch and then climbed up toward the top. Securing himself with rope and saddle, he lined himself up with the spot where he needed to make the jump cut. He had learned of 'jumping' the top from an old Frenchman named Marcel, who he had worked with at a previous tree company. Once the cut was done, he would tie another rope onto the top for the men below to pull it over. With that done, they would just notch the trunk and, hanging in his rope and saddle, Jeff would be ready to take down the crown of the tree and finally drop to the ground to control the taut line hitch.

The day was absolutely gorgeous; bright sun, clear skies, temperatures in the 70's. Fastened to his belt was a lightweight chainsaw that he would use to confidently jump cut the tree as he had done countless times before. However, just as he was about to pull the cord to start the chainsaw, he heard yelling and screaming. Looking around for the source of the noise, he saw the back of the top floor terrace and what appeared to be a man grabbing a woman and ripping her shirt. Before it could go any further, another man ran over, interrupting the assault. Jeff yelled down to Sam to call 9-1-1, saying it looked like there was a man beating on a woman on the third-floor terrace. He then saw the man running down the fire escape, jumping into what appeared to be a small, light blue Hyundai Tucson SUV.

"I'm going to make the cut," Jeff yelled, doing so and then tying the rope onto the cut end so they could pull it over after notching the trunk.

Jeff came down in his saddle, where he could see cops had arrived at the apartment building. It was then established that the man was trying to rape a young girl on the terrace, but it was interrupted by a maintenance man making his rounds. Of course, knowing he was up the tree to see everything and had been the one to tell Sam to call 9-1-1, the cops wanted to question Jeff. After learning that it was the third rape attempt in Kemper in the last year, he became suddenly hesitant about describing the vehicle, as it did look like his brother-in-law's. Of course, he knew it wasn't. A reporter also interviewed him, and he gave the same information as he had given the cops. The glaring sun had made it impossible to know exactly what it was other than a small SUV.

Around 3:30pm the crew got back to The Barn. Bert shared with Jeff, "We surely had enough excitement this morning. The chief told me that two rapes were reported on the South side of Kemper, and they think it was the same person."

"Yeah, I heard that too."

Joining them was Sam, who walked over, espousing, "Damn. After all this, I need a drink. What say you, gentlemen?"

Bert laughed. "I would love to, but I quit three years ago. My wife would scalp me."

Soon Sam and Jeff were in the Backside Tavern. Sam downed his shot and beer while Jeff clutched his Bud Light, saying, "This is my favorite part of the day."

"Amen. I agree."

The next day, a Saturday, Jeff took the day off to refresh himself, but the same thought seemed to play in his head. The SUV of that fleeing rapist looked like the SUV his brother-in-law drove.

That's crazy, he thought. Rick has been married to his

sister for at least 11 years, they have two small boys, and he knew his sister Shelly had always been crazy about him. So why is he thinking about this?

Then he thought of the striking 30-ish woman named Emma he had met at a going away party for a cousin who had joined the Navy. After several dances he asked her out and she agreed, but she canceled because of a bad cold, though not the flu or COVID. Since it had been a couple of weeks, he called her to see how she was doing. Answering, she told him that she was a lot better and was still on board with Jeff's invitation for dinner at an Italian restaurant on the edge of Seaburg. He picked it knowing she was Italian. They settled on Monday night for their rescheduled date.

CHAPTER TWO

GETTING HOME MONDAY NIGHT FROM a busy day of work, Jeff jumped in the shower to spruce himself up. They met at the restaurant on the south side of Seaburg. After a brief greeting, they entered the cozy little establishment together. Jeff couldn't take his eyes off of her. Everything about her was kick-ass, so to speak. Shiny, brown, flowing hair with sparkling deep-brown eyes, she wore a wraparound skirt, red blouse, boots, and dangling earrings that brought a warm glow to her radiant face. All of this, of course, coming together on a dynamite figure.

As he scanned the menu, Emma spoke, "I've been here a couple of times; everything is so good and fresh!"

"Yes, I heard good things about this place!"

Emma ordered a pasta dish and a generous mixed salad with extra olives. Jeff ordered a ravioli plate with garlic bread. Immediately after ordering he began to second guess whether it was wise to go for garlic when he might have a chance at a kiss afterward. *Stupid!* he thought.

Emma requested Zinfandel while he got his usual Bud Light.

Sipping her wine, Emma said over her glass, "You and your company had quite a stir recently. It was on the news and all over Facebook."

"Yeah, they think it might be tied to other rape attacks from the last two or three years… So, what do you do for work, Emma?"

"Oh, I work for the Registry of Motor Vehicles."

"That's cool," he said with raised brows.

"Yup, I enjoy the job."

"That's 95% of the experience," Jeff remarked. He knew he had to find out a little more about the lovely woman sitting across from him.

"So, what do you do for excitement?" he asked.

Emma tilted her head back a bit, looking upward. "Actually, not much since my ex-boyfriend, Tony, and I split. What about you, Mr. Hero Tree-Climber?"

Jeff laughed, "No hero, that was the maintenance man."

He followed with, "Not too much. I usually work six days a week."

"That must be strenuous work climbing those big trees."

"Well actually, Casey usually does most of the climbing so it's not too bad."

After they had a delicious meal, they walked out to Jeff's truck.

"Jeff, I had a great time. You have a way about you that I really enjoyed."

Jeff blinked. "I do?"

Emma smiled, not saying anything.

As she walked to her car, Jeff called out, "Do you think we could get together again?"

She looked back over a shoulder at him.

"Yes," she said, "maybe we can get together again."

"Okay, Emma, thanks for coming out tonight!"

She turned and walked back over to him, squeezing his arm and laughing.

"I've got a tree-climbing Tarzan with real gentleman vibes here," she said, turning again to get into her BMW convertible.

"Hey," Jeff called out, "I love your car!"

She just smiled wide and sped off, filling the air with the throaty roar of the engine. Jeff couldn't believe it. She seemed so reserved, yet he could feel the telltale signs that she perhaps had a sexy, wild inner-self. But would she really call him or was that a way of dissing him on a one-time date? Usually, isn't it the man that calls the lady?

CHAPTER THREE

A COUPLE OF DAYS LATER, HE stopped over at his sister's place after work. Shelly welcomed him, saying, "How's the ever-vigilant tree man?"

"Yeah, I know. I guess I had a bird's eye view..."

Then the two four-year old's, Joey and Conner, ran over, showing him their toys.

"Hey guys!" Looking over them and turning back to his sister, Jeff asked, "Where's Rick?"

"Oh, I asked him to pick up a few things at the market after work."

About a half an hour had passed when Shelly picked up her cell phone, telling her brother, "That's him, he's on his way."

Rick soon opened the door with a couple of bags in-hand. The boys ran over, happy to see him. Jeff said, How goes it/

"Not bad, how about yourself?"

"Actually, great news! My boss was impressed with the way I cataloged all the heavy equipment in our sales brochure."

Rick had been a salesman at Kenline Heavy Equipment in Ruxford for a while now.

"Looks like I might be up for a raise!"

"That's great with your growing family," Jeff was quick to say.

Shelly walked over, giving Rick a hug.

"You had some excitement at the job the other day," Rick said, continuing, "How about a beer?"

"Sure," Jeff replied.

"Jeffey, why don't you stay for dinner?" Shelly asked.

"Thanks, Sis, but I want to finish up the Chinese food from last night."

As Shelly turned to start preparing dinner, Rick and Jeff left the kitchen and headed into the small den.

"So, tell me more about your tree-climbing experience," Rick prompted.

Jeff recalled the story for his brother-in-law, going over all the details for what seemed like the millionth time.

"According to the reports, you couldn't quite make out the details for a full description because of the glaring sunlight."

"Yeah, that's true, but I don't think I could see that much because it just happened so fast."

Rick nodded before adding, "The maintenance man, I read, couldn't give a definitive description either."

"Yeah, I guess he was slowed down a great deal due to walking with a limp and being 74; just a little too slow to get over and get a good look. He yelled loud enough though that he scared off the attacker, who was masked anyway. The poor woman was so traumatized. All she said was it was a white man, maybe average height, wearing dark clothes."

"Damn!" Rick raised his voice. "Who the hell would think a small town like Kemper would have a rapist running around? That usually happens in the big cities."

"Not really," Jeff remarked. "Remember the Golden State Killer?"

Rick took a big swallow of his beer. "You didn't see his car?"

"Vaguely looked like a small SUV," Jeff shrugged, not letting his true thoughts show.

Rick chuckled, "There's tons of them everywhere."

With little more conversation, Jeff departed, walking by Rick's Hyundai Tucson, pausing briefly as he thought it must be merely a coincidence.

CHAPTER FOUR

THE FOLLOWING DAY, A SUNDAY, Jeff called up his long-time friend, Vince Ozzo, to shoot pool over at the Backside Tavern. As they were shooting pool, Jeff could hear people talking about the rape attack. Vince nudged him.

"Jeff, that's all I am hearing in this place. Do any of these people even know you at all?"

"I doubt it, it's a different crowd on weekends."

After doing a number on his friend at the pool table, Vince wanted to smoke a joint and said, "There's a party going on at Buddy O'Shea's. You game?"

"Come on, Vin. You know there's bad blood between me and him."

"Dude, I know, but you guys duking it out over that Rhode Island broad from Brown University, that was over three years ago now."

"Yeah, fighting over her and then she threw both of us under the bus. Damn snatch!"

Vin pointed to their vehicles, saying, "Come on, Jeff, just be cool about it."

Soon they could see several vehicles lined up around the driveway. Inside there was around fifteen people, mostly drinking or smoking pot, while in the corner there were three people huddled around a bong.

O'Shea walked over, saying mockingly, "Ozzo, you brought my old friend Standish. What a pleasure."

Jeff stood his ground making sure his words cut above the man's, saying, "What's up, Buddy!"

They were loud and loaded, staring at each other. Vince quickly lit his joint, saying to O'Shea, "Want a hit?"

O'Shea walked over, taking a hit, then saying, "Hey Jeff, grab yourself a beer in the barrel in the kitchen."

Jeff felt the tension diffusing as he and Vince saw a couple of friends sitting and smoking around a card table and joined them. Jeff loved his beer, but he kept away from any smoking, no matter what it was. Climbing trees, he needed clear lungs. Unfortunately, he also knew that secondhand smoke was just as bad or maybe worse.

After an hour or so, he told Vince that he was pushing off. Vince, of course, knew he had had enough of the thick air and carcinogens. He remembered the term from when he recently read about secondhand smoke, but himself, for some reason, he didn't give a fuck. *I'll die when I die.* While most everyone was in a somewhat inebriated state of mind, Jeff slipped out and headed home.

CHAPTER FIVE

IN THE MIDDLE OF THE week as he was getting ready for work, Jeff overheard the reporter on the TV. detailing another incident of rape near the center of town. Jeff shook his head, thinking about his brother-in-law, unable to rid himself of the feeling of uncertainty. Of course, it wasn't him. He just had to be sure... He had to find a way to eliminate all doubt about his SUV.

A couple of days went by, and Jeff began seeing and hearing more details about the rape on Facebook and the news. It had taken place in the oldest part of town called the Dye Factory section, so named because it was the home of one of the biggest dye factories and manufacturers of clothing dye in the 1920's and 1930's. It had eventually been converted into a shoe factory during a time when the shoe business was booming in Massachusetts especially. The buildings in the area had mostly been demolished long ago, including a second, expansion dye factory in West Bridgewater off Matfield ST. Jeff recalled when he got his first car and he would race around with a few buddies, burning rubber and hotdogging through the roads that connected around the complex. The shoe factory would take rubber waste that had been pauperized and put it in barrels outside on the property. Years ago, it was cleaned up by the EPA, but preceding that a few barrels rusted and the rubber, essentially rubber dust, would blow around and stick to the tires when it was wet. Curiosity drove him to see if maybe it could still be blowing around, escaping the grass, like it did years ago sticking onto his old Mustang.

After last night's rain and driving around, Jeff checked the tires on his pickup. They were clean. *So much for that theory,* he thought. If nothing had stuck onto his tires, surely nothing would have been on the rapist's tires if he drove through here. Of course, he knew he was just trying to eliminate his brother-in-law's Hyundai.

Returning to his pad, his cell rang; it was Emma asking if he was interested in going to a movie. Of course, he jumped at that. *Wow,* he thought, *I wasn't really sure I would see her again.*

Friday night finally came around and he picked her up at her townhouse at the Tangerine Apartments and headed to the theater. After seeing *Elvis*, which they both thoroughly enjoyed, they went to a small pub called the Green Half Onion, grabbing a booth.

"How's the job going?" Emma asked.

"Not bad. Today we planted some evergreens at a new CVS in Kemper. How goes the RMV?"

"Pretty good. Busy all the time."

Then Emma excused herself to the powder room, and he watched as she floated across the pub in a short, yellow sundress, draped with a lightweight vest. Her taste in jewelry was spot on; a silver bracelet, two rings – one gold and the other holding a birthstone. He got a hold of the table as an erection was trying to push through his summer cargo shorts. Grimacing, he hoped it would relax before she got back.

After enjoying great meals and drinks, Emma asked, "So what do you think, tree-climbing man, do you want to go to my nest to help me finish a Pina Colada mix I opened last night?"

"Sounds good," Jeff smiled.

CHAPTER SIX

SOON THEY WERE AT HER townhouse, and Jeff was impressed by how nicely she had fixed the place up.

Emma pointed. "Take a seat, I'll mix us up a couple of Coladas."

Jeff sat on the loveseat. Emma put the drinks on the small table, saying, "I am really into wine, but what the hell, rum is good too."

"Ditto. I am with you on that. For me, it's beer, rum, and once in a while a Chivas Regal Scotch.

"I made some coconut cookies. Would you like one?"

Jeff laughed, "Well, I never had cookies with rum."

Emma giggled, "I guess I wanted to see if you liked them. Cooking isn't exactly my greatest skill."

"Sure, that would be a tasty treat," said Jeff. He was in a desirable way and tried his best to hide it.

Emma got up to make them a couple more drinks and Jeff could feel he likely had a reddish beam, likely from blood pressure. *Slow down*, he thought, as he focused on her butt. She came back, sitting a little closer this time.

"Your bathroom?" he asked.

"Oh, two doors on the left."

His rising member was in half-way mode. In the bathroom, he splashed some cold water on his face, thinking, *If I get too forward on our first date, she might think I'm only interested in getting her to put out.* He had to play it cool on this. It was like having a stick of candy in front of him when he was a kid; all he wanted was to lick it, and lick it, and lick it some more.

After her third drink, Emma giggled, got up, then came back over with a short clothesline rope.

What the hell! Jeff thought.

Emma smiled, "You know, Jeff, when I was a teen, my Uncle Bob would invite my family for an outing on the Cape in Harwich. I was always fascinated with his boat lines and the way he secured them to the piers and all the different knots he and the other boaters used. I always wanted him to show me some of those knots, but there was never much time. Plus, I felt weird. Why would a 16-year-old care about that?"

"Really a bit unusual," Jeff remarked. "Maybe you thought some day you might have your own boat."

"Could be," Emma replied. "I loved the whole scene; the beach, boating, Cape Cod." She laughed, "Checking out the boys…"

"There you go," Jeff chuckled. "My father had a big maple taken down years ago at the house on Long Island, and I was watching the workers the whole time."

"So… You want to show me a few knots?"

"No problem, I was in the Navy for three years, and, of course, in my work we use them all the time."

"Sure, I would love to know."

Emma got closer as he showed her a half hitch, a running bow line, then a figure eight, a barrel knot, a clove hitch, a sheepshank, and a few more. Emma reached over, placing her hand on his arm.

"Let's go into my bedroom. We'll have much more room for you to show me your expertise in knots…"

Emma seemed more than eager. Jeff blinked and answered a long, "OK."

In her room, the bed was ample enough for his, he laughed at the thought, "teaching assignment". Of course, he knew otherwise. She grabbed him, unbuttoning his shirt.

"Mr. Tree Climber, I want you to tie me to the bed and make love to me."

Jeff was stunned. "You're serious?"

"One hundred percent," she purred.

"Okay then, I'll have to cut the rope into four different pieces. Do you want me to show you what kind of knots I'm going to use?"

Emma said nothing as he cut the rope with his jack knife.

"Wow," she said. "That's a pretty fancy knife you've got there."

"Yeah, it's a custom Buck knife."

Then he embraced her, helping her out of her clothes. Quantifying a long sigh, he said, "Emma, you're gorgeous, and you must work out."

"I do. Three times a week at the gym." She stopped him for a moment. "Are you okay with this?"

"Oh, I am, Emma, and don't worry, I would never hurt you."

He kissed her lips and neck as she tugged his pants down and said, "Get your duds off."

He then tied her wrists and ankles to the four bed posts using clove hitches. Next, he just went ballistic on her body, touching, licking, lapping, running his penis all over her. She was moaning in her private world of bondage as the muscular tree climber ran rough shod over her bound, helpless, captive, naked body. After at least twenty minutes, as Jeff couldn't stop caressing and kissing her perky breasts, he entered her with his tongue and her low sighs took on a higher pitch. He slipped his cock into her and what happened next was extraordinarily exhilarating to say the least, as she let out a scream.

"Oh, Jeff! Please don't stop!"

Then he painted her body again and began sucking on her nipples as she arched her back, breasts rising, and she let everything go. Hearing her, he couldn't keep his own firestorm from erupting.

Quickly, Jeff untied her as Emma went into the bathroom to pull herself together. Jeff just crawled under the sheets. Soon Emma came out in a robe, discarding it as she got under the sheets, her face a pinkish red.

"Jeff, I really lost it. I think you rubbed my G-spot."

He just rubbed her butt, saying, "I could do this seven days a week."

She laughed, "Boyfriend, I wouldn't be able to walk for a week."

He smiled, "I went from a date to a boyfriend?"

"Oh, yes. You don't think I'm letting you loose, do you?"

That last comment left him with a million-dollar smile. Then they planned on taking a relaxing nap, when Emma confessed, somewhat sheepishly, "Do you think bondage is maybe, er, kinky, sick, or maybe only people who do it are sexually dangerous?"

"Not at all, sexy lady. It depends who does it, and it all comes down to trust."

Emma hugged him. "Boyfriend, I knew I could trust you."

Jeff put his chest into her breasts. "Come on, baby, just relax and take a nap while I caress your derriere."

CHAPTER SEVEN

H E AWOKE AROUND 6A.M., THEN quietly donned his attire and tiptoed out the door to his pickup, looking back once as Emma was sleeping like a baby, thinking he never knew a woman who was into bondage, and, to put it mildly, it really turned him on. It now seemed to him that Emma was more than a beautiful woman, that she had at least a few layers of complexities, and like an onion, he would have to peel them all back to really get to know her.

At work, Sam, jumping in the crew cab with Jeff, remarked, "How was the weekend?"

"I've got to say, it was a hot weekend with my date."

Sam chuckled, "Oh yeah? How hot?"

Jeff smiled, "Sizzling hot."

A few days later he picked up his cell as it rang; it was his sister. "Hi Jeff! If you're not busy Saturday night, I'm having a potluck dinner at the house with a few friends and neighbors. Join us if you can. You know most of them."

"Sure, Sis. How's the kids?"

"Oh, they're fine," his sister said, as he heard them fighting in the background.

Shelly laughed, "Joey's trying to take a toy away from Conner."

Jeff laughed along with her, "May the strongest tyke win."

"Allright," Shelly said, "I'll see you this weekend."

Saturday quickly arrived. Jeff thought he might call up Emma to see how she was doing, but she wasn't able to talk much. The Registry was having an audit and she was straight out. So, with all said and done, Jeff drove to his sister's house.

Four of the neighbors were already there when the rest began arriving.

Turning to his sister, Jeff said, "Shelly, what time does Rick usually get home?"

"Oh, he called me about half an hour ago. He had to go into Boston to get a part for a Case front-end loader."

Eight o'clock rolled around when Jeff voiced, "I'm going to head out."

"You're not going to wait for Rick?"

"I think he got tied up in the Boston Saturday night traffic. Besides I want to stop by my girlfriend's place.

Shelly smiled, "Girlfriend? You didn't tell me!"

"Oh, well, it's just the opening chapter."

Shelly grinned more, "Okay, well, I'll tell him you were here."

CHAPTER EIGHT

JEFF THOUGHT HE WOULD JUST drive by and call Emma but not tell her he was in the area, knowing she was probably beat from the audit. He didn't want to press it but maybe she would ask him to come up. As the road went around the bend toward her apartment, he pulled in front of the townhouse and shock hit him in the head. Parked in the common driveway next to her was a light blue 2013 Hyundai Tucson SUV. Panicking thoughts crashed against his brain. Was it Rick's or the rapist? He quickly pulled up away from her front window. He had to call her to make sure she was alone. A few seconds went by, and Emma finally answered.

"Oh, hi, Jeff."

"Just a wellness call on account of the audit," Jeff breathed, relieved to hear her voice but not wanting to cause any worry.

"Oh, I am fine. Just beat from all the paperwork. We only have a couple more days of the audit, then everything will be back to normal."

"Okay, Sexy, just checking."

"Alright, Sweetheart, I'll be in touch."

Then Jeff drove a bit and got out to walk over into the shadows to take a picture of the registration with his phone. But before he could realize what was happening, the headlights came on and the Hyundai pulled out.

"Shit!" he exclaimed. *Could it be Rick's or the rapist's? Maybe just another 2013 Hyundai. Could be someone visiting?*

Returning to his pad, Jeff kept abreast of any news on the rapist. However, he knew he had to go back to his sister's place at some point to take a picture of Rick's plate.

The next day, he knew he had to find an excuse to visit his sister, so he found one and called up Shelly.

"Hey, how's the mother of those two hellions?"

"Yeah," she laughed, "they can be a handful. So, what's up?"

"I've had a hankering for lobster, and I know you and Rick love them, so how about I grab a couple for each of us?"

"Jeff, honey, they're so expensive now!"

"Don't worry, Sis. You game?"

"Come on over, say around six, and I'll have the water boiling."

Soon, Jeff was there with the lobsters, ready to bring

them inside to the awaiting pot. Before he got out of his pickup, he snapped a picture of his brother-in-law's plate, then made his way inside.

After lobsters and beers, he went with Rick into the den, which Rick always referred to as his own little man cave.

As he downed his brew, Rick said, "I missed you last night. The traffic was a real bitch getting out of the city."

"That's no lie," Jeff agreed. "Traffic everywhere since the pandemic calmed down."

"Shelly says you've got a new girlfriend. Anybody I know?" Rick conversed.

"You wouldn't know her; she's originally from Long Island, New York."

"Really? So, how's it going with her?"

"Well, not bad, but she works for the RMV and they're doing an intensive audit, so I haven't seen much of her lately," Jeff said before changing the subject. "Say, Rick, I saw a big scratch on the rear quarter of the Hyundai."

Rick shook his head. "Yeah, happened the other night when Shelly was at the mall. Some idiot backed into her."

After a few more beers, Jeff departed, thinking to himself, *I have the plate number so I can officially clear my suspicions of him.*

CHAPTER NINE

A LITTLE LATER DURING THE WEEK, Vince Ozzo called, eager to run the table with his skill at pool, which of course, he did, before relaxing at the bar with Jeff.

"How's it going with that registry broad?" Vince asked.

"Great, Vin. She's doing an audit, but it's winding down. Then hopefully she will invite me over."

"So, buddy, you got into her pants yet?"

Jeff pushed him. "Damn, Vin, you got to be so damn nosy!"

Laughing, Vin just said, "Know you, you wouldn't miss a score."

"Well, yeah we did, and she's one hot babe."

"She got a sister?" Vin said, only half-joking.

"I think so, but her family lives on Long Island."

Fast track to Tuesday when he got a call from Emma, just as he was about to prune a tree.

"Hey, Tree Man, how are you? Are you working Saturday?

"Actually, I'm not. Things slowed down a bit."

"Maybe we could spend the day together."

"Emma, that would be great."

"Meet at my place, say about one. I'll make lunch."

"Will do!"

Saturday arrived and Emma made some tasty grilled cheese sandwiches on rye with dill pickles and chips.

Sitting at the table, Jeff remarked, "What do you mean you can't cook! These are scrumptious!"

"Oh, Jeff, they're only sandwiches!"

"I don't know, they're really good!"

Emma laughed, "Probably because I added paprika and a few other things."

Then she got up and brought out some eclairs, asking, "Another beer?"

"Sure!"

As she handed it to him, Jeff asked, "Who owns that classic 1959 Pontiac Bonneville parked in the driveway?"

"Oh, that belongs to Danny in Apartment 14. He and his father restored it."

"Yeah? What a beauty! And you know what else, Emma, it reminds me of another beauty... You!"

Emma smiled, grabbing his hand, and leading him to the bedroom, where she embraced him.

"Honey, I want you to make love to me," she said as she removed his shirt and took in his toned and muscular upper body. After discarding their clothes, they really got into it, finally becoming crest-stared like buoyancy in the fog of the climax.

She snuggled up to him, saying, "Tree-Climber, you know how to please a woman. My former boyfriend couldn't hold a candle to you."

Jeff just squeezed her tighter, saying, "Do you think I was gentle the other night when we had bondage?"

"Of course, honey. But, of course, you don't want to be too gentle because it would take away from your domineering hold on a helpless captive," she said. Then, reaching down and grabbing his now rebounded cock, she added, "Someday, when we have one whole day to spend together, I want you to play bondage again. You think you would like that?"

"Absolutely, I would love to."

"I don't know why I am like I am. I guess I feel like a rebel who doesn't follow the norm. I guess I like being a captive of a handsome warrior like you."

He reached over and kissed her nipple.

"Honey, tell me what you would do to me, and don't hold back. I want to hear it all, Tree-Swinging Man."

"Well, after slowly taking off all your clothes, I would

tie you like before, using clove hitch knots, this time a little tighter than before. I would make sure you knew that you are my captive and are totally at my mercy. Then, I would shed my clothes, giving you a lustful, long look, and I would at first lick and lap each side of your stretched, naked body, but with more zeal than before."

Emma, looking up, was imagining she could see an intense sexual warrior in a high-octane demeanor. Suddenly she called out, "Wait, Jeff! No more! I'm getting that crazy feeling again and I don't want to waste it on make-believe."

"But, Honey, you told me to tell you what I would do."

"I know, I know. I'm sorry, but I'm getting too worked up, and I can't handle it. I want to save it for when it really happens, when we can spend hours playing our kind of playing house."

Jeff could see the beads of sweat on her brow.

"Okay, sweet lady, we can save it until it happens."

"Come on, hon, I'll make you a drink or grab you a beer if you prefer. The Cowboys are set to play the Raiders. Let's get dressed and I'll make some snacks and munchies."

After the game that Emma's favorite team, the Cowboys, won, Jeff pushed off, saying, "I've got to meet my buddy Vince for pool."

"Okay, sweetheart. Call me during the week."

Then, after a long embrace and kiss, he headed to meet Vince Ozzo.

CHAPTER TEN

I N THE MIDDLE OF THE week, there was another rape on the edge of Seaburg. Jeff found out that the police from three towns put together a task force. However, an elderly woman saw a glance of the supposed car that she saw two men run out after the assault and got in, maybe a Honda or a Toyota. Jeff thought, *I bet it was the Tucson, but two men?*

A day later, arriving at The Barn, Bert walked over.

"We got a job here in town over on Kingman Road. That's only a few miles. A rotted Sycamore Tree and we got some brush cutting. Today should be a breeze."

Arriving at the job, Jeff knew he was only about maybe a mile from the Tangerine Townhouses where Emma lived. On site, looking at the old Sycamore, he thought the tree really must be quite old to be dying, as a general rule they are extremely durable, and also called the American Plane Tree. It was sad that the tree probably sat for decades and would soon be no more.

Noontime arrived and the crew piled in the Dodge crew cab to go to Bub's Subs, only about five miles away. As they were heading for the Sub shop, he, of course, would pass Emma's townhouse. A light blue Hyundai Tucson was parked out front as he got a quick glance of the scratch on the side, cementing that, without any doubt, it was Rick's. On the way back from getting subs the car was still there. When the crew got back to The Barn, after dumping the chips into a pile, they all departed. However, once more, Jeff decided to go past the townhouse.

He saw Emma's BMW parked beside the Tucson. *She has ample places to park, why next to his car? Is she fucking him? Or maybe he tied her to the bed or perhaps she tied him to the bed in all its glory?* He was in so much despair that he pulled over to the side of the road. *My mind isn't weighing all of the facts. I really can't accuse anybody without proof.* He knew he had to go to his sister's again.

Two days later, Emma called. He told her he wasn't feeling great, that he thought it was a cold, so he would take some cold medicine, hoping she bought into the lie in order for him to gather his thoughts. With all that said and done, he headed for his sister's because an opportunity came up when it was his nephew Conner's birthday. He went to a toy store and bought him an Army tank. As he arrived, he saw that Conner had some of his neighborhood friends over. After Shelly cut the cake for her son's fifth birthday, everyone sat down to eat cake and ice cream.

Rick motioned Jeff into the den with two beers.

"How goes it with the girlfriend?" Rick said, handing him a Bud Light.

"Pretty good, she's a sweetheart. By the way, a couple of days ago we were doing a job on Kingman Road, and we decided to go to Bub's Subs for lunch. We drove by the Tangerine Townhouses, and I saw your car parked there."

Rick kind of gasped. "My car? Er, no." But he quickly corrected himself. "Oh, yeah. I was visiting an old high school buddy."

"No kidding. It must have been a long visit. Your car was still there on the way back from lunch. And, come to think of it, it was there when I went back to the sub shop for salad and pizza at 4:30."

Rick became visibly irritated. "What are you driving at?"

"Nothing, just making conversation."

Rick explained, "I had the afternoon off, so I went over."

"Hey pal," Jeff emphasized, "You don't have to explain anything to me. Why would I care?"

Jeff left shortly thereafter. *He knew I was onto him. Whatever it was. Maybe he was telling the truth, or was he visiting some gal pal? Or Emma?* Consternation ran rampant in his mind.

CHAPTER ELEVEN

T WO DAYS LATER, HE CALLED Emma. She embraced the call, "Oh, Jeffey, I was worried you caught more than a cold!"

"No worries, sweet cheeks. I'm good. Just wanted to know when we can get together again?"

"Say, Thursday night sounds good. You like Chinese?"

"Definitely."

"How about Chicago Chow Mein? Spareribs and fried rice?"

Jeff laughed, "Do cowboys love to go to a rodeo?"

"That sounds like a strong 'yes'. Come over around six."

"Okay, will do."

Jeff parked beside her car. Getting out, he took in the sleek lines of the Beamer Convertible, thinking, *Boy, the Registry must be paying her good money to afford payments of that baby.* And he always heard the Tangerine Townhouses were high caliber with high caliber rents to match. Then he noticed someone polishing the Bonneville, so he walked over.

"Nice car!" Jeff said by way of greeting.

"Yeah, me and my son restored it a while back," said the man.

"I just love those old cars. Now it's cookie cutter SUV's everywhere."

"I'm Henry, by the way. This is the second one I've done. The first was a '47 Buick that I sold for a hefty profit."

"Wow," Jeff retorted, "that's cool. It's good to meet you."

"Same here, er—"

"Jeff," he said. A fast-moving storm was coming in with heavy thunder and lightning, running off to join Emma.

"Wow, it's coming down hard!" Emma said."

"It came quick. Henry over there in the parking lot was waxing the classic Pontiac right before it hit. He must be bullshit."

"Well, anyway," Emma smiled, "I'm glad I got the Chinese food before the storm."

Jeff could see she was already lit from the Pina Coladas.

"Oh," she pointed out, "I got a six-pack of the Bud Lights you love."

"Thanks, Honey."

After eating their food, the weather seemed to be getting even worse, so Emma turned on The Weather Channel when a deep boom sounded, followed by a flash that lit up the sky.

"Damn," Jeff said. "Must be a transformer that blew."

Axillary lights came on, but they were really dim.

Emma kind of staggered, saying, "Jeff-a-roo, I know you're not into pot. Would you mind if I lit up a joint?"

"Of course not. I didn't know you used it."

"Now and then... Especially, when my hunky boyfriend comes over," she said, stumbling into his arms.

Jeff made her sit on the couch. "Damn, darling, how many Coladas have you had?"

She cracked, "You know, I lost count." Then, fumbling in her pocketbook, saying, "Fuck, I can't find my lighter."

After practically destroying her handbag, she pointed to the hutch. "Honey-Babe, will you check to see if there is one there?" Then, adding, "I don't know what I did with the flashlight."

"It's okay, Em," he said, as he put a small pillow beneath her to support her wavy head. "I carry a utility knife tool with everything from a light to a screwdriver."

Then, as Emma seemed to be drifting off, he went into every drawer, but no lighter. As he was about to close the last drawer, he noticed a small compartment built into it. Opening it, he saw that there was a gold badge. Bringing it out, he was floored when he read the description, "Detective Emma Compagno, Boston Police" followed by a number. For a few seconds he felt like he had lockjaw. *I can't believe it!*

By now, Emma had passed out. He just removed her shoes and covered her with a blanket, thinking she wouldn't be using any lighter even if he did find one. It must have been a couple hours that she was in Never Never Land. He left her a little note and decided he might as well go home and try to sort out his discovery that is girlfriend is a cop!.

CHAPTER TWELVE

When he got home, the lights were restored, and he hit the hay. Of course, now Emma became a mystery as well, on top of what his brother-in-law was up to. *Maybe she's working undercover on some kind of fraud at the registry? Damn.* Life just got complicated. Before, the only thing complicated was trying to figure out where he could meet the opposite sex, who would walk, talk, smile, dance, jump, and grin, each one emitting they own sexy appeal that would warm his soul. *And now that I am finally in love with a woman, will it all come crashing down?*

Saturday night rolled around, and Jeff and Vince were shooting pool at the Backside Tavern, when he said, "Hey, I know you work at a computer repair shop. Do you guys have any police radios for sale?"

"As a matter of fact, we've got a couple. Not the digital

ones, but they still scan pretty good. I repaired them a while back. Why?"

"I just want to follow any news of the rapist."

"Okay then, stop over Monday night."

"Okay, Vin. Sounds good," Jeff said, as his cell began ringing. It was Emma.

"Hi, Honey. I got your note, and I apologize for passing out on you."

"It's okay, Em. I guess you really got into those Pina Coladas."

"I guess I did, hon," she laughed. "Believe me, boyfriend, I paid big time in the morning. Where are you now?"

"Oh, me and my buddy are playing pool at the Backside."

"Say, I was wondering if you can come over tomorrow night? I'll stick to coffee this time."

"Seven okay?" Jeff laughed.

"Perfect," she answered.

After the call, Jeff thought to himself, *I am now in a tenuous situation knowing she's a cop. Somehow, I must keep quiet on this, so I don't upset the apple cart, so to speak. Maybe if she knows I know, perhaps it would change everything. But I can't take that chance when risking it might mean that what we have as lovers would be no more.*

Jeff shook his head, attempting to clear the thoughts from his mind, and returned his focus to pool. He had been improving lately. Vin was no longer slaughtering him entirely. He actually one two of their nine games this time.

CHAPTER THIRTEEN

S UNDAY ROLLED AROUND AND JEFF was trying to decide whether or not to say something about Emma being a cop. That night, his Ford 150 pickup was abreast of her white BMW. He chuckled to himself as he looked at the two vehicles side by side. *Me, the tree-climber, having torrid sex with a Boston detective. It's so wild, it's hard to believe.* His thoughts were interrupted as he arrived at her door.

"Welcome, Mr. Tree Climber," Emma smiled, as she opened the door. "Coffee or a beer?"

Jeff grinned from ear to ear. "I'll have coffee."

"How do you like it?"

"Cream and three sugars, unless you can fit in the cup."

"Oh my God, Jeffey, you're something else!"

After more mundane conversation, Emma grabbed his hand, giggling, "Come forth, Mr. Standish, into my Chick Cave."

"Hey, I like that," Jeff declared.

"Well, you know I missed you."

Jeff's eyes and grin told her it was mutual.

"Jump in bed," she said, pointing, "while I go into the powder room. And get out of your clothes!"

Jeff was transfixed on the bathroom when Emma came out in a sexy negligee. He gasped and was unable to say anything.

"I bought this for you, Tarzan of the apes. Do you like it?"

"Like it? I just want to peel it off."

She slipped under the sheets, snuggling next to him. For the next forty-five minutes he slowly bared her of the negligee, kissing every part of her, not missing one single freckle. He could tell she wanted him to sate her love channel, so he did in a thrusting firestorm, as she grabbed his buttocks and finally, he surged up inside of her like the eruption of Mount Vesuvius itself!

"Jeff," she whimpered, "what do you eat? barrels of Wheat Germ every day?"

"Hardly," he laughed, "but I eat it with my cereal a lot."

Then she said, "I heard you yell out. Did I elevate your rush higher than any tree you've ever climbed?"

"Oh, yes, babe. Higher than a Majestic Redwood."

"Oh, Jeff, you really floor me with the stuff you come out with."

After hours under the sheets, kissing and feeling, Jeff knew Monday morning was coming soon. They both agreed to rendezvous Wednesday night.

Monday night, a breaking report flashed across all the newscasts, telling of another rape, this time in Rumford. This time, however, the victim's boyfriend came home unexpectedly, and he and the girl were both shot. The boyfriend died instantly, and the woman died later at the hospital, but not before reporting that it had been two men who had raped her. Now the task force was looking for perhaps two killers.

CHAPTER FOURTEEN

Wednesday night came, and Emma called Jeff, letting him know she had some loose ends to tie up at the Registry and she wouldn't be able to make their date. Jeff wondered if she might be working with the task force full-time on these rape cases. As his mind wandered more, he further questioned the situation.

Is Emma being with me just as a way of relieving stress from all this or am I just thinking crazy things? I've got to figure out where Rick was on Monday night... But I've got to play coy on this, I don't want to tip him off...

The following afternoon he rang his sister. "Hey, Sis! I've got a jacket that needs mending. Wondering if you could mend it for me?"

"Of course, silly brother! You know I always mend your clothes. Come over at six and have dinner with us, and I'll take care of it."

"Thanks, Shelly. I can't resist your tasty meals."

"I'll tell the boys you're coming over."

Jeff thought to himself, *God, I hope Rick was home last night. Sure, he can be obnoxious at times, but a rapist? And now a killer? I hope the fuck not.*

Thinking about the events within the last few days, he realized he had forgotten to stop at the computer shop on Monday night to check out the police radios. So, before heading to his sister's place, he stopped by the shop. Walking in, a bifocal ed man was at the desk.

Jeff said, "Hi, my buddy Vin,, said you guys get police radios in now and then and you might have a couple for sale?"

"Correct," said the man. "But we don't have any digital."

"That's okay."

Then, as the man showed him one then another, they heard a police radio sounding from the nearby office and walked over to take a look.

"Maybe he repaired another. Let's check it out."

As they entered the office, they saw a police radio on a small table in the corner.

"I guess he has his own digital radio. Never heard it in here before."

Jeff offered, "Probably keeping up with all the crazy crime reports we've had lately, what with the rapist and all."

"Yeah, you're probably right. Do you want one of the others? Vin repaired them a while back; they should be good."

"Okay, I'll take the newest of the two."

Walking out of the store with his purchase, Jeff couldn't help but think it was a little unusual that his had a separate police radio in his office, but it was true he could have just been keeping up with it like everyone else.

CHAPTER FIFTEEN

Jeff arrived at Shelly's and saw Rick standing on the lawn, talking to a contractor.

Inside, Shelly said, "Rick wants to put an addition on the house, and he's looking for info."

"Yeah, with your growing family, it's probably a good idea."

Shelly motioned for her brother to sit down, then, looking out the window, said "I'll grab you a beer."

As she quickly rejoined him, she quietly said, "Jeff, I've got to talk to you about something important." Her eyes appeared to water as she pulled up a chair for herself. "Rick is going out a lot; he's always going somewhere. First, it's to put down bets at Roony's, then to his high school buddy, Rodger's. Sometimes he says he wants to finish a repair at work. I just have a lousy feeling that he might be cheating on me..."

Jeff stood up. "Did he tell you where his high school buddy lives?"

"All he said was he has an apartment at the Beacon Housing Complex."

Jeff shook his head, glancing out the window, saying, "I don't feel good on this, Sis. Beacon is a low-income development, but that's not where he's going. You know where the Tangerine Townhouses are on Kingman Road?"

"Yes, of course. Aren't they high rents?"

"Exactly, Sis. My girlfriend lives there."

Shelly's shoulders dropped. Looking dejectedly up at her brother, she said, "You saw him?"

"Well, not exactly. But I've seen his car there a couple of times. I even told him one day that I thought I had seen his car there as I was doing a job nearby, and he told me he was visiting an old classmate, just as you said. Just not *where* you said."

"Do you believe him?" Shelly asked, teary-eyed.

"Why did he say Beacon Apartments and not Tangerine? Something's not right."

Just then, Rick came in to share his ambitious plans for the new addition.

Around 7:30pm, Jeff left to head home, but ended up driving around attempting to clear his head and sort everything out. By 10:30pm, he was driving slowly by the Tangerine Townhouses, and, lo and behold, the Hyundai Tucson was back in the driveway. Driving down the street a bit, he parked and quietly made his way the short distance back, over to a small park adjacent to the townhouse, where he hid behind a large pine tree. Luckily, the full moon gave off plenty of light for him to see clearly when Rick walked out with a young, high-heeled woman to get into the SUV.

What a snake! He silently cursed. *What's he up to? Is he leading or tricking this young girl into something sinister? Maybe he is just a cheat and they're going to a club or a bar.*

CHAPTER SIXTEEN

THE NEXT NIGHT, VINCE OZZO rang him, saying, "Hey buddy! Your pool game is improving, and I can't have that. Let's get together and I'll really clean your clock this time."

"Tough words, pal. I'll see you in twenty," Jeff chuckled.

Driving up, he could see Vin's Red 2018 Dodge Charger. It was gorgeous; 3.6-liter V6, chrome wheels, and, as a finishing touch, skull valve caps. He was parked in front of the big window and alarmed to the teeth; no one would be taking this beauty from Vince. Jeff thought to himself how, despite being the same age, he was driving a pickup and his friend was driving *that. Damn, I'd never tell him, but I am so fucking jealous.*

Inside, Vin was already in a game with an older

gentleman. Nodding in greeting, Vin said, "You can play me as soon as I finish off John here."

"Confident as ever, aren't you, Vin?" John said, watching as John started making a comeback.

"Ha!" John laughed. "Nothing like fighting words to get me going!"

They got down to the eight ball when Vince had a fairly easy shot for the win; he was licking his chops, so to speak, in anticipation. However, he didn't quite put enough power behind his shot for it to go in, leaving John to finish him off. Jeff watched as John basked in his win, laughing, "First time all afternoon I beat him!"

Jeff smiled, "Don't worry yourself none. You whipped Vin and ended his reign of terror."

Vin countered, "But not for you!"

After John left, Vin said, "I heard on the radio in the car that the rapist struck again here in Seaburg near the Industrial Park."

Jeff was completely surprised. "Damn, I didn't hear that."

"Yeah. Someone better catch that bastard soon."

"How's the victim?"

"I don't know, but I didn't hear she was killed," Vince said, as he took the game five to three.

Returning home, Jeff decided to switch on the 10 o'clock news, where a reporter was saying that the rape was called into 9-1-1 at 8:30pm and the woman was taken to Seaburg Medical Center. Police would continue to comb the area for clues. Jeff thought to himself, *This guy must be a psycho, and the police can't catch him.*

Jeff jumped in the shower, continuing to mull over the reporter's words. *Wait a minute. I got to the pool hall at 7:45 tonight, and Vin told me about the latest rape before it was even 8 o'clock. The reporter on the news said it had been called in at 8:30... How would Vin have known before the cops? Maybe there was an error in the reporting or I just misheard it?*

CHAPTER SEVENTEEN

LATER IN THE WEEK, EMMA invited him up for a 7 o'clock dinner at her place. Jeff wondered what might be on the menu. She had mentioned before she thought herself a lousy cook, so maybe she ordered takeout. When Jeff got to her door, he was stunned as he took in her short, wraparound, red dress, complimented by a black blouse and flat white shoes.

"Damn, Em. You should have told me you were going to knock me out with that getup. I would have dressed up."

Emma beamed. "Oh, we had a conference at work with state officials, so I just spruced up a little when I got home." She kissed him and added, "No sense for you to dress up because before you leave you will be in your Tarzan attire anyway."

Jeff cracked, "That's next to nothing."

Emma gave him a pearly white smile, ear to ear,

in response. "Okay, now sit down; I got us a bottle of champagne."

"What's the occasion, babe?"

"Honey, it's my birthday."

Jeff reeled back. "What?! Why didn't you tell me?!"

"Well, I guess I got so busy at work that I just forgot."

Jeff walked over to her, "Honey, that's no excuse. I have to confess, I got it real bad for you, but I always worry that someday you won't be here."

"Why do you say that?"

"I guess the only fairy-tales I believe in are the ones with bad endings."

Emma sighed, saying, "Oh, Jeff. I'm not going anywhere."

Just then, the intercom buzzed; the catering company had arrived to deliver two prime rib dinners with all the fixings, cake, candles, and everything.

"My parents and sister wanted me to come home to Long Island, but I couldn't right now," Emma said.

After finishing a truly remarkable meal and polishing off the bottle of champagne, Emma pulled a joint from her purse.

"What do you say, hunky boyfriend? Do you want to share a joint with me for my birthday?"

"Honey, where did you get that stuff?"

"Relax, hon, I bought them at a cannabis dispensary. I would never buy them anywhere other than there.

Especially with all the Fentanyl coming over the Southern Border."

"Okay, then I will, just for your birthday." Jeff said before adding, "I'm getting you something for your birthday too."

"That's okay, Jeff," Emma said, looking at his crotch, "You can give me something later."

Then, just as before, she couldn't find her lighter. "You can tell I seldom smoke. Did I have you check the hutch before?"

"You did, Em. No lighter, just your detective badge…"

Her face dropped. "You saw it?"

"Don't worry, it's all on the Q.T."

"Honey," she looked at him pointedly, "I'm pretty sure I can trust you. Am I right?"

"Honey, you know you can or you wouldn't let me practice my skill with knots."

She chuckled, "Well, yeah… It all comes down to a woman's intuition."

Jeff pined, "I don't need to know anything more."

Emma pointed, "Sit at the table," as she took a seat across from him.

"I was sent to the Seaburg Registry to investigate Cyber Fraud and a network of stolen registration plates and interstate of identities in Mass and Rhode Island."

"Damn, Em, you got a lot on your plate."

She continued further, "When the rapes started

happening, my superiors put me on the task force to track the vehicle down that the rapist was seen driving."

Jeff got up, looking like he was holding something back.

"What is it, Jeff?"

"Well, I saw the car, and I know exactly what it is."

Emma looked dumbfounded. "But the report just said you saw a small SUV."

"I did. And the make. And the model. And the color..."

"Go on," she said with a raised brow.

"It was a 2013 Hyundai Tucson SUV, light blue. I didn't say anything because my brother-in-law owns one."

Emma sighed, saying, "You want a beer?"

"Yes please."

She looked at him intently as she handed him the beer and nodded for him to continue.

"So, I did some checking on his whereabouts. Of course, I never believed it was his, but in my mind, I had to eliminate him. I found out he was cheating on my sister. Whoever he's cheating with, she lives here at the Tangerine."

"How do you know that?"

Jeff continued, "One day working a job near here, we went to a sub shop on lunch, and I saw his car parked over here. That night I hid in the park I saw him with a young girl, all dressed to kill, high heels, reddish blonde hair, walking out with him and getting into his car."

"A hooker?"

"I don't know, Em."

"Does your sister know anything?"

"I had to tell her what I knew."

"Well now," Emma said, "we have a description of the car. It's the break we have been looking for. Jeff, you know your brother-in-law has to be investigated."

"Yeah, I know. Surely it wasn't him though. He might be having an affair, but raping and killing people?"

"Darling, I am sure you're right. This information won't be put out to the press right away, at least not until we check out any Tucson of that description. It would only be put out if we draw blanks. If that information got out too early, the person or persons responsible could destroy it, maybe burn it."

"Yeah, but wouldn't you have the person's name on the registration?"

"While that may be true, there are a lot of ifs in investigations, and there might be evidence inside that car linking to all of these attacks. We don't want the person behind all this to know that we know what he's driving."

Jeff then put forth, "The million-dollar question then… Are you going to say I told you?"

"Not at first. I'll say it was an anonymous tip to start,

but down the road I might have to. Don't worry, I'll protect you."

So, after further conversation and, of course, lovemaking, he went home. *I know*, he thought, *I am right about Rick. God, at least I hope I am.*

CHAPTER EIGHTEEN

AGAIN, IN THE POOL HALL with Vince, Jeff recalled when he first met him several years ago. Vince had told him he was from Lincoln, Nebraska and was dating a girl from there pretty seriously. When she told him she enrolled in Boston College and would have to leave, Vin promised to visit. And while he did, the girl ended up meeting someone else and dissing him. Being a cracker-jack repairman when it came to computers, Vince had gotten a job in Seaburg and stuck around ever since.

Rousing Jeff from his memories, Vince asked, "Still banging the registry chick?"

"Of course, she's my girlfriend."

Vin just laughed.

"What about you? How's it going with the chick you met at the computer shop?"

"So far so good. We have a date Friday night."

"Oh yeah? What's her name?"

"Megan. She works for Kemper Financial."

"No shit. Another computer whiz?" Jeff grinned.

"I don't know, but she's got an awesome ass."

CHAPTER NINETEEN

BACK ON THE JOB, THE crew took down two maples and a small cedar tree that too many insects had gotten into. Jeff climbed both maples due to Casey being sick. Returning to The Barn, Jeff and Sam Parker decided to head to the Blackside.

Sam said, "Buddy, you must be beat. That was a tough day."

"Yeah, I am," Jeff replied, snickering, "Maybe I can get my chick to give me a back rub."

"Still hot and heavy, huh?"

He smiled, "More than that, Sam. I got it bad for the broad."

Sam downed his shot. "Women!" he laughed, "They can really wreak havoc sometimes! Years ago, my old girlfriend started demanding all kinds of things, especially money, or I would have to sleep on the couch."

Jeff chuckled, "So, what happened?"

"I'll tell you what happened. I finally gave her walking papers," Sam said as he clutched his shot glass of Jack Daniels. "Old Jack doesn't give me any crap, so we have a pretty good relationship."

Jeff threw his arm around his friend, saying, "You set her right, huh, Sam?"

"That I did, buddy. But after I threw her out, I missed her."

Jeff quipped, "You know the old saying; can't live with them, can't live without them."

Later in the week, he called Emma to ask her out to a fancy restaurant, to celebrate her birthday on him this time.

"Oh Jeff, come on now. My birthday is over. I don't want you to be spending money on me."

"I want to. Case closed, Miss Emma."

"Alright, Tree Man, when?"

"You tell me whenever you can."

"Okay, a week from this Saturday would be fine," she said. "Oh, hey. I know you love my car, so how about I let you drive us there in it?"

"That's awesome, I've never driven a BMW!"

"I am sure you'll like it."

CHAPTER TWENTY

THEIR DATE ROLLED AROUND, AND Jeff, for the first time in a long time, donned a sports jacket and cleaned up especially nice for her. He still couldn't believe his luck as he drove the Beamer, with its throaty sound and surging power. Emma's perfume drifted under his nose as they drove. This was it; this was the Holy Grail. Awesome car. Beautiful Boston detective.

After arriving at the restaurant, they both decided on the filet minion. Emma requested a Manhattan, while Jeff called for a ginger-based beer. After a few minutes savoring their drinks, Emma began sharing an update.

"Honey, we've been checking 2013 Tucson's here and in Rhode Island, and there's still a few on the radar. There are four in the Seaburg/Kemper area and another also in Parkfield. So far, everyone has checked out with the task force. It seems, though, that one owner took it off the road a couple of years ago. No record where it went."

"What do you mean?" Jeff asked.

"The person simply traded on in at Kemper Hyundai for a Dodge Charger, but nobody knows what happened to the car. That was two or three years ago."

"Well," Jeff said, "a lot of times the dealers will sell trade-ins to smaller, used car lots for short money. Sometimes they'll just sell it for parts if the mileage is too high." Suddenly, it dawned on him that Vince had a Charger. "Em, what year Charger?"

"I don't know, hon. Later when we get back to my place, I'll check the reports."

Back at Emma's townhouse, she dug through the reports.

"It says here, Vince Ozzo trad—" They both gasped. "Oh my God, that's your friend!"

Jeff put his hand over his face. "My best friend."

"Honey," she said, "that doesn't mean anything. Like you said, the dealers probably sold it to a car lot. It was more than likely sloppy bookkeeping."

"Could be," Jeff said, still rattled. "I'm sure you're right."

"How long have you known him?" Emma asked.

"I think three, maybe four, years. He's from Lincoln, Nebraska. Chased a girl up to Boston when she got into Boston College. Then she dumped him."

CHAPTER TWENTY-ONE

THE NEXT DAY, JEFF CALLED Vince to ask if he was up for pool.

"I'm always ready!"

After several brews and a few games, Jeff asked, "You must have played a lot in Nebraska if you're this good?"

"Yeah, that we did. Drive fast cars, chase loose women, and shoot pool. There was a pool hall not far from me, and a bunch of us would meet and sometimes bet on games."

"Say," Jeff inquired, "what weight stick do you use?"

"Twenty ounces."

"Still with the new girl?" Jeff asked.

"Of course."

Jeff spoke as he chalked his cue stick. "Looks like you've done alright for yourself since coming east. Got a great job, nice car, cool pad, and a new girlfriend with an 'awesome ass'. I got to admit, I love that Charger of yours. Did you drive it all the way out here?"

"Oh, no. I bought it here. I took the bus from Lincoln. I couldn't afford anything like that back then."

Then, after a night of Jeff nearly winning and Vin continually winning, they headed to the bar stools.

"Listen," Jeff began, "tomorrow, I want another shot at you. I ordered a new cue. Should be here by tomorrow night. You game?"

"Sorry, Jeff. For once, I'm out. Megan and I are going to a dance club in town."

"That's alright, we'll have a rematch when you're free. It'll give me time to practice with the new cue anyway."

"Buddy boy," Vin smiled, "a new cue won't do you a lick of good. I got your number!"

"Ha ha," Jeff laughed, "that's what Custer said about the Indians."

CHAPTER TWENTY-TWO

ON THE WAY HOME, JEFF'S mind was racing. *I've got to put to rest my suspicion that Vin might be involved in this, just like I did for Rick. It seems like he's taking Megan out, but I'm not even sure she exists. He's always talking and bragging about women, but never brings any around. We're best friends, you'd think I would have met at least one.*

On his way home, he stopped at a drug store to pick up a few things, when he called out, "Hey Kidzze!" It was Lana Berry, who most knew as Kidzze. He recalled their brief relationship when he was nineteen.

"How are you, Jeff?"

"Not bad. You're looking good. How's it going?"

"Great, I got married a couples of years ago."

"Anybody I know?"

"You wouldn't know him, he's from Texas. Matt Evans."

"No kidding."

"Yeah, and we've got one on the way."

"That's great!" he said, as he thought back to the apartment she had lived in years before that had once been occupied by bank robbers, who, rumors claimed, had hidden much of their stolen money in the walls.

"Anything new?" Kidzze asked.

"Nothing earth-shattering."

After more light conversation, she departed, leaving him thinking fondly back on when they had tapped on the walls all across her apartment in hopes of finding the rumored treasure but were always stopping for romps in the bedroom!!

CHAPTER TWENTY-THREE

IN A SMALL CAFE ON the edge of Seaburg, Vin Ozzo pulled in and joined Howard Dunbar.

"Vin," Howard said, "I think it's time we ended this."

"What?! We got the copes baffled!"

"That's true, but this task force... I think we should cut out."

"Howie, it's working out great with you being a tech expert and getting all this info on these women, tracking their movements, their addresses, finding out about any roommates, getting all their schedules. It makes robbing them a breeze!"Vince laughed, "Taking turns banging the bitches is just icing on the cake. In fact, I think that redhead you scored on was the CDO of that big lumber company."

"No, Vin. I really think we should stop. I've got a

bad feeling. Remember the B.T.K. killer in Kansas? He stopped and started again, and then they nabbed him."

Vin thought for a moment. "Alright, but I want one more score. And this one I picked out myself."

"What do you mean?"

"She's my so-called buddy's girlfriend. Her name is Emma. Saw her with him a while back and she's a real looker. All I need you to do is unlock the Tucson from your garage."

"I don't know…"

"Come on, Howie! You owe me! And don't forget it was YOU that shot that couple."

"Is that a threat?"

"No, just making a point."

"Alright, fine. This is the last time. Then we have to burn the Tucson."

CHAPTER TWENTY-FOUR

MEANWHILE ON THE OTHER SIDE of town, Emma was worrying about her tree-climber. *Poor Jeff! He's so stressed out about his best friend. I know he plays pool over at the Backside, and Jeff said he's always there drinking. Maybe I can find out if he's involved with a little ruse. He wouldn't know me from Eve....*

After talking to Jeff, who was headed over to his sister's house for dinner, Emma drove over to the Backside Tavern. Inside, it was fairly crowded, as they were having a meat raffle in the room off from the bar area. She went to the bar and ordered a drink. While she had never seen him before, Emma had a feeling that the man sitting right at the end of the bar was Vince.

Vince was shocked to look up and find her walking into the tavern. *What's she doing here? Looking for Jeff?*

After a little while, he moved down the bar to sit next to her.

"Hello. Haven't seen you around here before. You here for the meat raffle?"

"I am, but I like my Margaritas better."

"Hey, that's great," Vin laughed, as someone put a new song on the jukebox. "You like to dance miss…?"

"Julie."

Vin already began scheming. *I don't need the Tucson. And anybody that knows me is already at the raffle.*

"You like to dance, miss Julie?"

"Okay," Emma obliged, as put his arm around her, drawing her in close.

If I can get her in my car after I slip a mickey into her drink, I definitely won't need the Tucson.

A guy walked over, looking at Vince. "What, no pool tonight?"

"Can't you see I'm busy?" Vin brushed him off.

"Say, you dance pretty well. What's your name?"

"Billy," Vin replied, thinking he'd need to get her out of here before someone used his real name.

Back at the bar following their dance, Emma excused herself to use the restroom. Vin took the opportunity and slipped Choral Hydrate, the making of a mickey, into her drink.

In the bathroom, Emma wondered how she might get

him to open up, either to incriminate himself or to take the suspicion off of him and put Jeff's concerns to rest.

After a few more drinks, with the meat raffle nearing its end, Vin was determined to get her out before everyone came flooding back into the bar.

"Come on, Julie. Looks like the booze hit you hard," he said, as he helped her out the door and over to his car.

CHAPTER TWENTY-FIVE

SHELLY'S SISTER-IN-LAW, WENDY, WHO WON a meat bag, was walking to her car when she caught sight of Vince helping a woman she'd never seen before into his Charger. On the way home, she stopped at Shelly's to tell her she won the $400 meat raffle.

"That's great!" Shelly, Rick, and Jeff all congratulated her.

"Hey, Jeff, I saw your buddy helping a woman that seemed like she had a few too many drinks. Then I remembered that Shelly said your girlfriend drives a BMW convertible. There was one parked right next to Vin's car.

Jeff's eyes opened wide. "What?" he said, stunned. "You saw Vince?"

"I did. Opening his passenger door, helping some woman who looked like she was inebriated."

"Come on, Jeff, let's take my car!" Rick said.

"No!" Wendy cried out. "Your car's too slow! Take my Camaro!"

They roared over to the Blackside, where they found the BMW still parked. Jeff jumped out, telling Rick he had a spare key to his girlfriend's car.

"Rick, I think she might be in serious trouble. You'd better stay here. I've got to do this alone."

"You might need help!"

"No, Rick. This could very well be a kidnapping."

Rick looked perplexed. "Should I call the cops?"

"No, that might not be a good idea. Emma could be harmed. Please, just let me handle it. I think I know where he's going." Jeff quickly jumped behind the wheel of the Beamer. "I'll be in touch!" he called, speeding away, grateful he'd been carrying his .38 Smith & Wesson revolver this night. Jeff raced to Vince's apartment, no Charger in sight. Now he was certain he knew where they had gone.

At top speed, the sports car entered the Dye Factory Area, hoping his hunch was right and he would get there in time. *Fuck!* he thought. *Vince must be the rapist!* He remembered a while back that Vince had mentioned exploring the ruins of the complex because he was curious of its history. Likely another bullshit story, manufactured to cover his tracks. *But why Emma?* He broke into a cold sweat at the thought that he might be too late.

Nobody knows the ruins better than me, he reminded himself. Riding bikes and exploring every building, every shed. Then, as a teen, he had raced his Mustang around the roads that encircled the huge dye and shoe factories.

CHAPTER TWENTY-SIX

VINCE PULLED BEHIND A SMALL concrete shed, which, last year, he and Howie had taken a young girl behind and gang-raped before they dumped her back at the area where they first found her hitchhiking. The shed was less decrepit than the buildings around it. Vince opened the door, grabbing a limp Emma, and dragging her inside. He just finished tying her wrists to a metal chair when she started to come back around. Emma now knew her life was in danger.

"Well, my hottie, you're finally awake?" Vince said. "I thought you might like to join me for a little party, EMMA!" He smiled as the shock washed over her. "That's right. You weren't there for a meat raffle. I know you were looking for me, bitch!"

Vince got right in her face. "What, do you think I'm involved with the rapes?"

Emma eyed him defiantly. "It's not looking so great for you at the moment, all things tonight considered," she spat.

"Shut up, slut! Like I said, we're going to have a little party. And you're going to be the big star."

He went outside to his car, grabbing a bunch of rags. Returning, he said, "After I take all of your clothes off, I'll tie you to those iron rings on the floor. But, of course, I wouldn't want any insects to bite you, so the rags will be your bed. After all, the only thing that's going to be touching that gorgeous body of yours is my tongue." He gave a sinister cackle.

"Before that, I think I'll go through your purse and see how much money you brought me." He opened a zippered compartment in her bag, noticing her ID. "Ah, Miss Emma Compagno. Nothing personal that it's a one-way party—" He reeled back, cutting himself off as he found her badge. "You're a cop! Boston detective. So, that's why you came to the Blackside, to investigate me. Well, sister, you let your guard down. Now, are you ready to have some real fun?"

Suddenly, Vince saw headlights shining in the distance, likely just teenagers parkers, but he pulled a handgun from his waistband just in case and walked out the door.

Emma looked around for any way she might help herself. Checking the ties, she realized that the knots

Vince had used were the common square knots. Jeff had once told her those could be easily loosened by vigorously twisting them. Realizing the distraction from the headlights might be her only chance, she got to work on the knots.

CHAPTER TWENTY-SEVEN

JEFF AIMED FOR THE ONE area he thought they could be the only concrete structure still holding up. Gun in hand, he crept up, knowing immediately that the small alleyway would bring him to the side of the shed. Someone was walking toward him, holding a flashlight and a gun. It was Vince, he realized. Just as the man was about to open the door, Jeff yelled, "Vince!"

Vince whirled, preparing to fire his gun when a bullet from Jeff's own .38 hit him in the leg and he went down. Jeff ran over, kicking his gun away, then quickly opening the door. Behind it, he found Emma, free from her ties, holding a metal bar as if ready to strike.

Realizing it was him, she nearly sagged with relief. "Oh, thank God it's you!" She ran to him. As they embraced, she continued, "I was going to smash him over the head. Probably would have killed him."

"No loss there," Jeff responded.

"How did you find me?" Emma asked.

"I'll tell you later. But will you tie a tourniquet on his leg to stop the bleeding? That way real justice can be served."

She grabbed a rag from the pile he presented her as a bed and administered the tourniquet. Jeff struggled to catch a signal with his cell.

"Come on, Em. Grab his gun. Let's blow this place, and I'll call 9-1-1."

Soon, the police and the EMT's arrived, stabilizing, and handcuffing, Vince. He later confessed to the rapes and dimed out Howard Dunbar.

After, Emma said, "Honey, you were more of a cop than me at the ruins."

"Don't sell yourself short, babe. He had you drugged. You would have nailed him when he walked through that door though."

CHAPTER TWENTY-EIGHT

TEN YEARS PASSED AND JEFF recapped the events. Vince and Howard were given life sentences, plus ten years. His sister Shelly still could never trust her husband again, and they divorced, with Rick being allowed visiting rights to the boys. Burt, his foreman at the Cedar Post Tree Company retired. Casey returned to Ireland to join his cousins. Sam Parker eventually retired as well, but still frequents the Blackside Tavern, still clutching his friend, Jack Daniels. As for himself, He had gotten a job at the C.O.A. driving a van, bringing the elderly to and from their appointments. Getting away from tree-climbing relaxed his limbs, which had begun showing signs of Arthritis.

He thought back to a few weeks following those events ten years ago when he and Emma were relaxing with glasses of wine at her townhouse.

"Honey, my work here in Seaburg is done. They want me back in Boston," she said.

"Yeah, I figured that was coming," Jeff said, looking down.

Emma stood and gestured for him to do so as well, when she began, "I want you to take my apartment."

Jeff clenched his teeth. "I don't know, babe. I don't know if I can afford the rent."

She hugged him, "Don't worry, boyfriend. I am still paying it."

"Thank you, Emma, but that doesn't go for me. I wouldn't want you to pay the rent."

She ran her finger along his face, saying, "Jeff, I don't think you know this, but I'm in love with you."

"You are? I never would have thought."

"Why, hon? What do you mean?"

"Well, I don't know, I'm just a tree-climber, a woodcutter. Nothing special."

"Oh, yes, my man, you're special alright," she said, leading him into the bedroom.

"Emma, I have been in love with you almost since the beginning of all this."

"I know, I know," she said, shutting the door behind them.

For two years following that, he lived there at the Tangerine Townhouses, and Emma would come over as much as she could. For two years he had wondered if he would truly ever have a happily ever after, as Emma never mentioned marriage. He figured he would do what he had always done, live in the moment. His ancestor Myles Standish had prevailed and stood his ground in a new world, despite dangers around every corner. Now, here he was, different dangers troubling this Standish man; the danger that Emma could suddenly turn the switch off for her love for him.

But here they were, after ten years. They had booked a cruise to Italy, and now, as they were walking to board the ship, Jeff asked, "Honey, are you sure you didn't forget anything?"

Emma smiled, dangling a clothesline rope she had pulled from her handbag, "Not a thing, darling." Then he smiled too, wider than the Atlantic Ocean they would soon cross together.

Printed in the United States
by Baker & Taylor Publisher Services

Printed in the United States
by Baker & Taylor Publisher Services